Zainab
the Squishy Toy
Fairy

By Daisy Meadows

ORCHARD

www.rainbowmagicbooks.co.uk

Jack Frost's
Ice Castle

Rachel's
House

TIPPINGTON
TOWN

Jack Frost's Spell

Every human child gets joy
From playing with a squishy toy.
No more, I say! Those days are gone.
I'll take their treasures – every one!

With Zainab's panda I'll grant my wish.
And own all toys that squash and squish.
I'll laugh out loud to hear her whine,
When all the rarest toys are MINE!

Contents

Chapter One
The Sponsored Squish

Tippington town square had never been so busy. Children were crowding together in front of the mayor, and grown-ups were squeezed in behind them. There were long tables all around the edges of the square, covered with "Squash-Mee" capsules. They were the most popular collectible toy of the year, and each one had a squishy character hiding inside.

"Welcome to Tippington's very first sponsored squish," boomed the mayor. "You've all been sponsored by friends and family to find out how many Squash-Mees you can open in five minutes. All the money we raise will be given to Tippington Children's Centre."

"I can't believe how many people have turned up," said Rachel Walker, who was standing at one of the tables. "I have never seen so many Squash-Mees in one place!"

Rachel's best friend, Kirsty Tate, was sorting through the capsules.

"There are Squash-Mees from every film and TV show I can think of," she said. "This is going to be amazing. I'm so glad that you invited me to stay with you this half term."

They shared a happy smile. They had both filled their sponsorship forms with names.

"I wonder if the golden Squash-Mee is here somewhere," said Rachel, looking at the brightly coloured capsules.

The golden Squash-Mee was the rarest of all. Only one had been made, and every Squash-Mee collector in the country was longing to find it.

"Please find a place beside the tables," said Mayor Osborne. "The sponsored squish will be starting soon."

Rachel and Kirsty chose a spot at the end of a table and waited for the other children to find their places. Just then, Kirsty noticed something strange.

"That blue capsule looks as if it's been opened," she said, pointing.

Rachel reached out and picked it up.

"It doesn't feel as heavy as it should," she said. "The two halves haven't quite been pressed back together."

Kirsty let out a little squeak of excitement.

12

"Rachel, it's glowing," she said. "I think it's magic."

The girls knew all about magic. Together they had shared many adventures with their fairy friends, helping to stop Jack Frost and his mischievous goblins from causing trouble. Whenever they saw the magical glow of fairy dust, they knew that something wonderful was about to happen.

"We can't let anyone else see this," said Rachel. "Where can we hide?"

They had promised the queen of Fairyland never to tell anyone about the magical secret they shared. Kirsty glanced around and saw the statue of Tippington's first mayor at the side of the square.

"Let's duck down behind that," she said.

With the statue hiding them from sight, Rachel and Kirsty crouched over the little capsule. Rachel cradled it in her hands.

"It's trembling," she whispered. "I think it's going to hatch like an egg."

With a sound like tinkling bells, the two halves of the capsule fell apart, and out fluttered a tiny fairy. She was wearing

a red dress with a
pattern of white
flowers.

"Oh thank
goodness, I've found
you at last," she said
in a relieved voice.
"Hello, Rachel and
Kirsty. I'm Zainab
the Squishy Toy Fairy,
and I need your
help."

"What's wrong?"
Kirsty asked.

"Everything is
wrong," said Zainab,
flinging out her arms.
"This is the worst day
I've ever had."

"Try to calm down and tell us what's happened," said Rachel in a gentle voice. Zainab sat down with a little sniff.

"It's Jack Frost," she said. "Oh dear, oh dear, what am I going to do?"

"Zainab, if you explain what's wrong, I'm sure we can help you," Kirsty said.

Zainab flicked her wand and a tiny handkerchief, no bigger than Rachel's little fingernail, appeared in her hand. She kept sniffing into it as she talked.

"It's my job to look after squishy toys all around the world," she said. "I have a very special magical object to help me, called the squishy panda. It makes sure that squishy toys always bounce back into shape, and it keeps them safe."

Zainab dabbed at her eyes.

"Go on," said Rachel.

"This morning, there was a knock at my door," said Zainab. "I went to look, and no one was there. But when I came back inside, the window was open and my squishy panda had gone."

"Oh no," said Kirsty, her hand to her mouth. "I bet I know who it was!"

"Only one person is mean enough to do such a thing," said Zainab. "I flew to the window and saw Jack Frost zooming away on a thundercloud."

Chapter Two
A Disgruntled Goblin

A single tear rolled down Zainab's cheek and plopped on to Rachel's palm.

"We won't let Jack Frost get away with this," Rachel promised.

Just then, they heard cries of dismay coming from the town square.

"My Squash-Mee has gone all flat!"

"I twisted mine and it broke into two pieces."

"Mine won't rise back up again."

"Oh no," said Zainab with a groan. "This is all because Jack Frost has my magical object. Without it, squishy toys all over the world will be losing their squishiness and breaking."

"Everyone loves squishy toys," said Kirsty. "People have loads of fun collecting them and searching for the rare ones."

"We have to get Zainab's panda back before the sponsored squish starts," said Rachel.

"You mean you'll help me?" Zainab asked, drying her tears.

"Of course we will," said the girls together.

"But where do we start looking for Jack Frost?" Kirsty asked. "He could have gone anywhere."

Rachel peered around the statue.

"The grown-ups are giving some speeches," she said. "We've got a bit of time and no one's looking. Let's go to Fairyland and see if we can track him down together."

Zainab waved her wand, and little puffs

of coloured fairy dust burst and billowed around them. The girls instantly shrank to fairy size. As they unfurled their wings, the bright colours swirled into a rainbow of magical sparkles.

The whirlwind swept the three fairies up as quick as a wink, and carried them away. They had hardly got their breath back before they were tumbling over and over on soft, sweet-smelling grass. They stopped at last, surrounded by daisies and buttercups. Tiny toadstool houses were dotted all around them.

"We're back in Fairyland," said Kirsty
in delight.

The sky was deep blue, and fluffy white
clouds scudded across it. Rachel jumped
up and gazed around. In the far distance
she could see the sparkling ice mountains.

"Jack Frost's castle is that way," she said,
pointing. "Let's go and see if we can find
him."

The fairies zoomed away from the
sunlit hills. Soon they were speeding
across snowy woods, shivering under grey
clouds. Zainab used her magic to cast a
spell protecting them against the cold.

"Look down there," said Kirsty,
pointing.

A single goblin was tramping away
from the Ice Castle through the snow. The
fairies swooped down towards him.

"He looks grumpy," said Zainab. "I wonder what's wrong."

"Let's ask him," said Rachel.

She landed on the snow in front of the goblin. Kirsty and Zainab fluttered down on either side of her.

"Hello," said Rachel in a friendly voice. "Are you OK?"

"Go away and leave me alone," snapped the goblin. "Silly fairy."

"Why are you leaving the castle?" Kirsty asked. "Won't Jack Frost be cross?"

"He won't care," said the goblin, sticking out his bottom lip. "All he thinks about is Squash-Mees."

"What do you mean?" asked Zainab.

"He's got Squash-Mees on the brain," the goblin complained. "The whole castle is full of squishy toys. They're all over the place. He wants to find the golden Squash-Mee."

"So that's why he took my squishy panda," said Zainab. "He thinks it will help him to find any Squash-Mee he wants."

"This is terrible," said Kirsty. "Every time there's a rare Squash-Mee, he will take it. Collectors all around the world will lose their best finds."

"Worst of all, children's favourite toys will be taken away or broken," said Zainab. "We must stop him."

Rachel put her hands on the goblin's shoulders.

"If you help us, there won't be so many

Squash-Mees in the castle," she said.
"Please, tell us where to find the squishy
panda."

The goblin glared at her, and then
shrugged his shoulders.

"Jack Frost told us to go and hide
it somewhere," he said. "But the other
goblins wanted to go to the Tippington
Toy Bazaar."

"Oh, I love it there," said Rachel.

"Me too," said Zainab, waving her wand. "Let's go!"

Chapter Three
Tunnel Trap

There was a flurry of twinkling lights, and suddenly the fairies were fluttering against the ceiling of the Tippington Toy Bazaar.

"This is such a magical shop," said Zainab.

The whole shop was lit by warm,

flickering candlelight. Shadows wavered on the orange and blue walls. The shelves were carved with delicate patterns, and there were little dens and secret grottos hidden throughout the shop.

A tiny model railway track ran through the building, and a green steam train chugged along it every now and then. High up on the wall, hidden vents puffed out bubbles and glitter.

The toys on the shelves were just as exciting as the shop itself. There were mysterious painted boxes with secret drawers, little dolls with real eyelashes and their own wardrobes of clothes, music boxes lined with velvet, miniature cars with doors that really opened, and boats with working sails. There were clockwork ballerinas and tin soldiers, soft

teddies that growled when you pressed
their paws, hobby horses with flowing
manes, tiny drums and trumpets, and a
collection of jewel-coloured kites with
ribbons on their tails.

"That's my favourite place in the shop,"

said Rachel with a smile.

She pointed to a corner where the shelves were packed with pocket-money toys. There were trays of golden rings, boxes filled with yo-yos and wind-up mice, rows of skipping ropes and pots of dice, buttons and beads.

"Oh my goodness, we have to come back here when we're human again," said Kirsty. "But for now we need to look for the squishy toys. That's where we'll find the goblins."

The shop was filled with people, and the fairies stayed high above the crowds. They reached the squishy toys aisle and saw empty capsules and Squash-Mees everywhere.

"The goblins have definitely been here," said Kirsty. "But where are they now?"

"Look!" Rachel exclaimed.

A goblin was peering at them from
around the corner at the end of the aisle.
When he saw them staring, he squawked

and darted out of sight.

"Follow him!" cried Rachel.

They zoomed after the sprinting goblin. He raced along the aisles, sending people and toys flying all around him.

"He's leaving the shop," Zainab called.

Keeping their fingers crossed that no

one would look up, the fairies followed
the little green goblin as he crossed the
street and dived into a brightly coloured
building.

"That's the Soft Play Palace," said
Rachel in an excited voice. "I know my
way around here. I'm sure we can catch
up with him."

Inside, the fairies were tiny enough
to slip in through the netting. The
children were so busy rolling, sliding and
bouncing that none of them noticed
the little fairies. Rachel, Kirsty and
Zainab weaved in and out of the netting,
flitting from one level to another as they
searched.

"I can see a green leg sticking out of
the ball pit!" Kirsty called out.

The fairies swooped down to where

the large, green foot was waving around among the plastic balls. The balls were flung aside and a cross-looking goblin sat up.

"Who buried me?" he squawked, and then he spotted the fairies. "Fairy alert!"

He scrambled for the exit, jamming

a cap on his knobbly head. He was wearing shorts and a T-shirt, and with his head covered he looked just like a child.

"Follow him," said Zainab. "He could lead us to my squishy panda."

The fairies flitted back through the soft play, diving and darting out of the way of the children. The goblin tumbled down steps, whizzed down poles and zoomed along zip slides. But he couldn't shake the fairies off. At last they saw him sprint into a long, yellow tunnel.

"Now we've got him," said Zainab, panting. "I'll go to the other end and stop him. Maybe then he will answer some questions."

She flew to the other end of the tunnel, just as Rachel and Kirsty heard a familiar cackle of laughter from inside.

"Zainab, stop!" cried Rachel. "It's a trap!"

Kirsty darted forwards to peer inside the tunnel, just in time to see Jack Frost slam a net down over Zainab.

"Got you!" he said. "I'll lock you in my

dungeon until you tell me where to find the golden Squash-Mee – and how to work the squishy panda."

Then Jack Frost and Zainab disappeared in a flash of blue lightning.

Chapter Four
A Royal Visit

"We have to go to Fairyland and get help," said Kirsty.

Thanks to their gifts from Queen Titania, each of them had enough fairy dust for one trip to Fairyland. They opened their lockets and sprinkled the fairy dust over their heads. At once everything went blurry, and then they were standing exactly where they wanted to be – in the Fairyland Palace throne room.

"Where is everyone?" Rachel exclaimed.

The two thrones were empty. Not a single fairy or frog footman was in sight.

"Who will help us now?" groaned
Kirsty.

Just then, they heard a giggle, and
something started bouncing in the
corridor outside the throne room. Rachel
and Kirsty fluttered to the door and saw
Georgie the Royal
Prince Fairy playing
with a rubber ball.

"Georgie!" they cried.

The Royal Prince
Fairy gave a squeal
of delight and darted
forward to throw her
arms around them.

"It's wonderful to see
you both," she said.

"We came to see the
queen, but there's no one

here," Kirsty said.

"Yes, the queen and the king have gone to collect Princess Grace for a visit," said the Royal Prince Fairy. "I'm here to make sure that everything is perfect for the royal children."

"Georgie, can you help us?" asked Rachel, clasping her hands together. "Zainab is in terrible trouble."

Quickly, she and Kirsty explained what had happened. Georgie looked shocked.

"Have you heard of the golden Squash-Mee?" Kirsty asked.

"Yes, I have," said Georgie. "I've heard that there is only one in the whole world. Do you want me to find out where it is, so that you can tell Jack Frost and make him set Zainab free?"

"Georgie, are you offering to let Jack

46

Frost win?" asked Rachel.

Georgie let out a long sigh.

"Children love squishy toys," she said.
"It's not fair that Jack Frost should
be allowed to get them all and spoil
everyone's fun. But if giving him the
golden Squash-Mee is the only way

to rescue Zainab, then we have to do it. All the toys in the world are not as important as Zainab's freedom."

Rachel hung her head sadly, but Kirsty stood up very straight.

"No," she said in a stubborn voice. "Maybe there's a way to get Zainab and the squishy panda back without letting Jack Frost spoil things for children all over the world."

"What's your idea?" Georgie asked.

Kirsty turned to her in excitement.

"It's just like you said," she explained. "Jack Frost and his goblins seem to want all the toys in the world. If they get lots of toys, they might stop thinking about Zainab long enough for us to rescue her. Georgie, can you magic us to the Ice Castle and make toys appear there – lots and lots and lots of toys?"

Georgie winked at them and raised her wand.

Rachel and Kirsty wrapped their arms around their bodies, shivering. They had appeared outside Jack Frost's castle. A biting wind was whipping up tiny specks of ice that stung when they hit bare skin.

"Where are all the toys?" asked Rachel, looking around.

For a moment, Rachel and Kirsty wondered if Georgie's spell had gone wrong. Then something small and red fell into the snow in front of them with a loud WHUMP.

"It's a toy capsule," Kirsty exclaimed.

WHUMP! WHUMP! A green one and a blue one fell on either side of the little fairies.

"It's raining toys," said Rachel as more and more coloured capsules fell around them. "This is perfect."

Kirsty cupped her

hands around her mouth.

"Hey, you in there!" she shouted as loudly as she could. "Jack Frost! Goblins! We have come to get our friend back."

"Go away!" squawked a voice from the castle battlements.

"Don't you want to know what toys are inside these capsules?" Rachel called out. "They're just lying here, waiting to be opened."

Lots of goblin heads appeared at the battlements. They stared in wonder at the capsules, which were still raining down from the sky.

"These are a gift from Georgie the Royal Prince Fairy," Kirsty shouted to them.

One of the goblins shook his head so fast that it made his ears wobble.

"It's a nasty fairy trick," he said. "I bet all the capsules are empty.

"They're not," Rachel exclaimed, picking one up. "Look – see?"

She opened the capsule and held up a sparkly green goblin doll. The goblins oohed and ahhed.

"Just come and have a look," Kirsty called out. "I promise, there is a toy inside each capsule. And fairies never break a promise."

The goblins disappeared from the battlements. For a moment the castle seemed quiet and still. Then the large doors opened, and a gaggle of goblins streamed out. They raced towards Rachel and Kirsty and then fell to their knees, trying to gather as many capsules as possible. Some collected capsules

underneath them like eggs in a nest.
Others balanced capsules on heads,
shoulders and even noses. One tried to
tuck his under his chin, but they shot
out and hit another goblin in the back.
Squabbles broke out in every direction,
and tempers flared.

"This is our chance," Kirsty whispered.

Chapter Five
Deepest Dungeon and Tallest Tower

The large doors to the castle still stood open. Flying as low as possible, Rachel and Kirsty swooped away from the greedy goblins, across the frozen snow and into Jack Frost's castle.

The courtyard was empty. All the corridors that led off the courtyard looked dark and dangerous.

"Which way?" Rachel whispered.

"We have to find steps going down," said Kirsty.

"And we don't have much time," Rachel added. "As soon as the goblins have opened the capsules, they'll be coming back. Let's just pick a corridor and start looking for a way down."

They zoomed towards the nearest corridor. Then Rachel glanced down and grabbed Kirsty's hand.

"Look," she said, in an excited whisper.

Half hidden under damp straw, the fairies could see the wooden planks of a trapdoor. Their hearts thumped as they pushed the straw aside. There was a rope attached to the heavy ring-pull.

"We'll have to work as a team to lift

this," said Kirsty. "One ... two ... three ... heave!"

They pulled with all their strength. The trapdoor creaked, shifted and then fell open with a loud bang. The fairies didn't wait to see if anyone had noticed the noise. Side by side, they flew into the darkness.

At first, Rachel and Kirsty couldn't see anything. The blackness seemed to press all around them. There was a damp, musty smell in the air. They held hands and fluttered down until they felt stone beneath their feet.

"My eyes are starting to get used to the dark," said Rachel.

She could see a wall beside her, and she reached out her hand. It felt rough and wet under her fingers.

"Everything looks a little bit green," said Kirsty, rubbing her eyes. "I wonder why."

They folded their wings and tiptoed on a little way. They could hear a steady dripping noise and the green light was growing brighter. Rachel glanced up at the ceiling and let out a cry of alarm.

"What's that?" she exclaimed, forgetting to be quiet.

The ceiling was moving. Hundreds of wriggly, glowing shapes squiggled above them.

"I think they're glow worms," said Kirsty.

"Phew," said Rachel. "I think all the

hairs on the back of my neck stood up then!"

Suddenly, a trembling voice called out of the darkness.

"Rachel? Kirsty? Is that you?"

"Zainab!" they cried.

The path gave a sharp curve and opened out into a large space. Around it were four caves with black, barred gates. Zainab was standing inside the nearest cave.

"I'm so happy to see you," she said, laughing with relief.

"We're happy to see you too," said Kirsty. "But how are we going to get you out of there?"

"That's easy," said Zainab. "Jack Frost left my wand down here. He put it just out of reach to tease me."

She pointed to where her wand lay on
the stony ground. Rachel at once picked
it up and handed it to her. Smiling,
Zainab tapped it on the bars of her
prison cell, and the door melted into
nothing.

"Now we have to find the squishy panda," said Rachel.

Zainab's dark eyes flashed.

"I think I know where to look," she said. "Jack Frost told me that he was going to the tallest tower. He's still trying to find the golden Squash-Mee."

"Then we need to go to the tallest tower quickly," said Kirsty. "We have to get out of the dungeon before the goblins realise that we're down here."

Rachel and Kirsty led Zainab back along the dripping green corridor. They told her how Georgie had helped them to get into the castle.

"The squishy toy capsules will keep the goblins busy for a while," said Zainab. "Oh look – I can see daylight. I think it's the way out!"

Soon, all three fairies fluttered out through the trapdoor. To their relief, there were no goblins in sight.

"It's wonderful to breathe fresh air again," said Zainab.

Rachel was looking up at the towers of the castle. One of them was so tall that the tip disappeared into a snow cloud.

"That's the one," she said, pointing. "Let's fly up and try to find a way in."

Chapter Six
A Splendid Dive

Halfway up the tower, the fairies saw
a narrow window with no glass in it.
They flew inside and found themselves
standing on an ice staircase. Rachel put
her finger to her lips and led the way up
the winding steps.

There was a door at the top, and the

fairies paused and looked at each other.

"We have to go in," said Kirsty in a low voice.

"But Jack Frost will see us straight away," said Zainab. "He'll just disappear with the squishy panda again."

"Not if he thinks we're goblins," said Rachel.

With a wave of Zainab's wand, their fairy wings disappeared. Their skin turned green, their heads became bald and knobbly, and their feet grew to twice their usual size.

"Who's out there?" snapped Jack Frost's voice. "Stop messing around and come in. I can hear you whispering."

Kirsty felt Zainab trembling as she pushed open the door. The disguised fairies saw Jack Frost pacing around a stool in the middle of the room. On the stool was a sparkling squishy panda. Squash-Mee capsules covered the floor.

"What do you lot want?" Jack Frost snapped, glaring at them. "Did you bring my snack? Is it biscuits? You'd better not have forgotten the chocolate ones."

"We don't have your snack, my lord,"

squawked Rachel, stepping forward. "I'm sure it'll be here soon. Would you like us to look after your panda while you wait for your snack?"

"No I wouldn't," said Jack Frost. "Keep your bony hands off my things."

He took a step forward and then stared at Zainab.

"What are you doing with that fairy's wand?" he demanded.

"Uh-oh," said Kirsty under her breath.

She darted forwards to try to snatch the panda from the stool, but she wasn't quick enough. Jack Frost grabbed it and cackled with laughter.

"Too slow," he jeered. "You're not goblins."

Zainab flicked her wand, and their goblin disguises vanished.

"Please," she said quietly. "Please listen to me. I know all about looking for rare squishy toys. Searching for them is half the fun. If you cheat with the squishy panda, you won't enjoy the hunt so much."

"Rubbish," said Jack Frost.

"If you use magic to find out what's inside all the capsules, you'll miss out on the excitement of opening them," Rachel said. "I love that feeling."

"The only thing I care about is winning and being

the best," said Jack Frost. "Now tell me
how to find what I want, or I'll drop this
into the moat!"

He sprang over to the window and held
out Zainab's squishy panda.

"Please don't!" cried the little fairy.

At that moment, they heard the
sound of running footsteps. After that,
everything happened very quickly indeed.
A goblin burst into the room, shouting
that the fairy had escaped. Startled, Jack
Frost jumped . . . and let go of the squishy
panda. Everyone shouted "NO!"

Then Kirsty took a flying leap out
of the window and dived towards the
freezing waters of the moat. She flew as
fast as she could, reaching out her hand,
plunging downwards . . . and plucked the
squishy panda out of the air just before it

hit the water.

Rachel and Zainab, who had flown
out after her, hovered above and cheered,
while Jack Frost leaned out of the
window and yelled at them all. Kirsty
flew back up and put the squishy panda
in Zainab's hands.

"Thank you," said the fairy in a breathless voice. "Thank you for everything you've done. You've both been amazing."

"We're just glad we could help," said Rachel, beaming at her.

"You flying pests!" Jack Frost bellowed behind them, shaking his fist. "Goblin, fetch my wand!"

"We should go," exclaimed Kirsty.

"I'll send you back to your sponsored squish," Zainab said. "I'm going to find Georgie – I owe her a big thank you."

The fairies shared a final hug, and then Zainab waved her wand. Fairy dust twinkled around them, and when it cleared the girls were sitting behind the statue in Tippington's town square.

"And now, the moment you've all been waiting for," boomed the mayor's voice. "Take your places for the sponsored squish!"

Rachel and Kirsty scrambled to their feet and raced over to their table.

"Do you think one of us might discover the golden Squash-Mee?" Kirsty asked.

"I have no idea," said Rachel with a smile. "But it's going to be a lot of fun finding out!"

The End

Now it's time for Kirsty and
Rachel to help ...

Ivy the Worry Fairy

Read on for a sneak peek ...

"I can't believe we're both here," said
Rachel Walker.

"Me neither," said her best friend, Kirsty
Tate. "It was the best surprise ever when
we arrived last night and saw you."

It was Saturday morning, and the
girls were looking forward to a relaxing
weekend at the Olive House Family
Mindfulness Retreat.

"Our parents are pretty good at
keeping secrets," said Rachel, laughing.
"They planned for us to be here together,
and they didn't say a word about it."

The girls shared a very special secret of

their own. Ever since they had first met, they had been friends with the fairies. They had been to Fairyland many times, and were always ready to help the fairies foil bad-tempered Jack Frost and his naughty goblins.

"We even get to share a bedroom," said Kirsty.

She sat on her bed and bounced up and down. The room was pretty, with sunshine-yellow curtains and a vase of daffodils on the dressing table. The window looked out over the big garden of Olive House.

There was a knock on the door, and Rachel's mum came in with Kirsty's mum.

"Your dads have gone for an early walk and we're going to join the morning meditation class," said Mrs Walker. "Would you like to come?"

"Yes please," said Kirsty, jumping to her feet. "I want to try everything this weekend."

"Me too," said Rachel. "Josh made meditation sound amazing."

Josh was the Mindfulness Guide at Olive House. The girls had met him when they arrived the evening before.

"I thought so too," said Mrs Tate. "I hope I can be as calm and relaxed as Josh by the end of this weekend."

The meditation class was being held in the summerhouse in the garden. It was a sunny morning and birds were singing loudly in the leafy trees. When Rachel and Kirsty reached the summerhouse, they stopped in surprise. Josh was there, but he didn't look calm. His forehead was wrinkled with worry lines.

"Good morning, Josh," said Mrs Walker.

"I'm afraid it's not a very good morning so far," said Josh.

Read Ivy the Worry Fairy to find out what adventures are in store for Kirsty and Rachel!

Calling all parents, carers and teachers!
The Rainbow Magic fairies are here to help
your child enter the magical world of reading.
Whatever reading stage they are at, there's
a Rainbow Magic book for everyone!
Here is Lydia the Reading Fairy's guide to
supporting your child's journey at all levels.

Starting Out

(1) Our Rainbow Magic Beginner Readers are perfect for first-time readers who are just beginning to develop reading skills and confidence. Approved by teachers, they contain a full range of educational levelling, as well as lively full-colour illustrations.

Developing Readers

(2) Rainbow Magic Early Readers contain longer stories and wider vocabulary for building stamina and growing confidence. These are adaptations of our most popular Rainbow Magic stories, specially developed for younger readers in conjunction with an Early Years reading consultant, with full-colour illustrations.

Going Solo

(3) The Rainbow Magic chapter books – a mixture of series and one-off specials – contain accessible writing to encourage your child to venture into reading independently. These highly collectible and much-loved magical stories inspire a love of reading to last a lifetime.

www.rainbowmagicbooks.co.uk

"Rainbow Magic got my daughter reading chapter books. Great sparkly covers, cute fairies and traditional stories full of magic that she found impossible to put down" – Mother of Edie (6 years)

"Florence LOVES the Rainbow Magic books. She really enjoys reading now" – Mother of Florence (6 years)

The Rainbow Magic Reading Challenge

Well done, fairy friend – you have completed the book!
This book was worth 5 points.

See how far you have climbed on the
Reading Rainbow opposite.

The more books you read, the more points you will get,
and the closer you will be to becoming a Fairy Princess!

How to get your Reading Rainbow
1. Cut out the coin below
2. Go to the Rainbow Magic website
3. Download and print out your poster
4. Add your coin and climb up the Reading Rainbow!

There's all this and lots more at
www.rainbowmagicbooks.co.uk

You'll find activities, competitions, stories, a special
newsletter and complete profiles of all the
Rainbow Magic fairies. Find a fairy with your name!